For more than forty years,
Yearling has been the leading name
in classic and award-winning literature
for young readers.

Yearling books feature children's
favorite authors and characters,
providing dynamic stories of adventure,
humor, history, mystery, and fantasy.

Trust Yearling paperbacks to entertain,
inspire, and promote the love of reading
in all children.

OTHER YEARLING BOOKS
BY PATRICIA REILLY GIFF
YOU WILL ENJOY

PATRICIA REILLY GIFF

Number One
Kid

illustrated by
ALASDAIR BRIGHT

A YEARLING BOOK

This is a work of fiction. Names, characters, places, and incidents either are the product of the author's imagination or are used fictitiously. Any resemblance to actual persons, living or dead, events, or locales is entirely coincidental.

Text copyright © 2010 by Patricia Reilly Giff
Illustrations copyright © 2010 by Alasdair Bright

All rights reserved. Published in the United States by Yearling, an imprint of Random House Children's Books, a division of Random House, Inc., New York. Simultaneously published in hardcover in the United States by Wendy Lamb Books, an imprint of Random House Children's Books, a division of Random House, Inc., New York.

Yearling and the jumping horse design are registered trademarks of Random House, Inc.

Visit us on the Web! www.randomhouse.com/kids

Educators and librarians, for a variety of teaching tools, visit us at www.randomhouse.com/teachers

Library of Congress Cataloging-in-Publication Data
Giff, Patricia Reilly.
Number one kid / Patricia Reilly Giff ; illustrated by Alasdair Bright. — 1st ed.
p. cm.
Summary: When Mitchell's father gets a new job and his family moves, he and his sister go to a new school where they must make new friends and adjust to new routines.
ISBN 978-0-385-74687-8 (trade) — ISBN 978-0-385-90925-9 (lib. bdg.)
ISBN 978-0-553-49468-6 (pbk.) — ISBN 978-0-375-89635-4 (e-book)
[1. Schools—Fiction. 2. Brothers and sisters—Fiction. 3. Self-confidence—Fiction.] I. Bright, Alasdair, ill. II. Title.
PZ7.G3626Nu 2010
[Fic]—dc22
2009033019

Printed in the United States of America

10 9 8 7 6 5 4 3 2 1

First Yearling Edition

For Jillian Rose O'Meara,
our darling,
with love

Special thanks to Laura Giff and Jimmy Giff, who told me
stories of the afternoon center

—P.R.G.

• • •

For Helen and Harry

—A.B.

Yolanda

Sumiko

Charlie

Destiny

Gina

Mitchell

Habib

Clifton

Trevor

Terrible
Thomas

Angel

Peter

CHAPTER 1

FRIDAY

Mitchell McCabe looked up at the classroom clock.

Were the hands moving?

Maybe not.

School would never be over.

This was only the first week in his new school. A million weeks until next summer!

His teacher, Ms. Katz, was giving out

permission slips. "We are lucky to have an Afternoon Center at the Zelda A. Zigzag School," she said. "Take these slips home. Get them signed."

Afternoon Center? What was that?

"We'll have swimming and art and ballroom dancing." Ms. Katz poked at her glasses. "Trampoline, kickball. Lots of things, even homework help."

In the next seat, a girl was drawing something.

It looked like a pony, Mitchell thought.

It had a fat stomach and four legs.

The girl raised her hand. "How about trips? Maybe like the Bermuda Triangle. Or Hawaii."

Mitchell leaned forward.

Ms. Katz closed her eyes. "I don't think so, Yolanda."

Mitchell put his slip in his desk. No good. He wasn't going to the Center. It would be filled with kids he'd never seen before. Even sixth graders.

At last, the bell rang.

Mitchell sped down the hall.

He slid down the banister—

And landed on the floor.

Bonk!

"Careful," the principal called after him.

Mitchell leaped out the door. Free.

He looked back. The Zelda A. Zigzag School was long and low. The bricks were as yellow as a stick of butter.

It wasn't one bit like his old school. That one was tall, like a cereal box. It was red.

And friendly.

Too bad they'd had to move. Too bad his father had a new job.

A window opened on the second floor.

Ms. Katz leaned out.

One room down, another window opened. Was that his sister Angel's room?

Yes. Her head, her skinny neck, and even her shoulders hung out.

Mitchell hoped she wouldn't fall. She'd land on her mouse-tail hair. He opened his mouth. "Be care—"

Behind him, the doors banged open. Kindergarten kids came out. And some huge sixth graders.

"Hey, loser," a sixth grader called.

Upstairs, Ms. Katz snapped her fingers. "That's enough, Peter Petway."

Mitchell took a quick look at Peter Petway. He

was gigantic! Did Peter think he was a loser?

Mitchell dived behind a green bush. He landed on someone.

"Oof!" It was that boy from the class across the hall. The one with the hair that stuck up in front.

Two voices were calling, "Mitchell."

One was Ms. Katz's.

The other was Angel's.

"You forgot your permission slip, Mitchell," Ms. Katz said.

"He does stuff like that," Angel said. "He loses things. He forgets things. And he's supposed to walk home with me."

Mitchell shook his head. He'd forgotten that.

"I'll come get his slip," Angel told Ms. Katz.

Mitchell leaned against the bush. It was full of thorns. Ouch!

He swallowed. He wouldn't cry. Not even if a tarantula landed on his head.

Next to him, the boy was almost breathing on him. The boy's arm was a mess of poison ivy.

Mitchell took tiny breaths. He tried not to breathe in the poison.

Above them, both windows closed again.

Mitchell took a deep breath. Oops. Poison ivy must be twirling down his throat.

The kid scratched his arm. "I'm Habib. What are you doing here?"

Mitchell raised one shoulder. "I'm Mitchell. I like to sit behind bushes. But not poison ones. How about you?"

"I'm making mud balls. They're great to juggle."

Mitchell crawled around with Habib. They made a ton of mud balls.

Then Angel came out. She was with another girl.

It was someone from his class.

He tried to think.

The Bermuda Triangle girl. Yolanda. She lived on their street.

Yeeks!

He hoped she and Angel wouldn't be friends.

She might tell Angel everything that went on in his class-room.

His mother would find out if he did one thing wrong!

He waited for them to go down the street. "See you," he told Habib.

He followed Angel and Yolanda home, sneaking from bush to bush. . . .

He made sure they didn't see him.

He felt a worm of worry in his chest.

More than a worm. A snake of worry.

Was Peter Petway right?

Was he turning out to be a loser?

CHAPTER 2

MONDAY

The weekend was too short.

Monday was too long.

The afternoon bell rang.

Mitchell went down the hall. He trailed his fingers along the wall.

His thumb hit Zelda A. Zigzag's picture.

He stopped to straighten her up.

She had been the principal a hundred years ago.

"It's time for Afternoon Center," Angel said, "Down in the basement."

Mitchell sighed. "Go ahead. I'm coming in a minute."

"It'll be fun. If you pay attention to things." Angel sped away.

Mitchell went downstairs. He sat on the bottom step. He wasn't ready for the Afternoon Center.

Habib clattered down behind him. "I'm a first-class juggler." He threw two mud balls into the air.

They went flying—

Straight into the kindergarten shelf.

The shelf was filled with scribbly paper shapes. They went flying, too.

Poor Zelda had a crumpled-up face. She looked as tough as a wrestler.

She probably ate nails for lunch.

He tried to remember the new principal's name. He snapped his fingers. Mr. Rand, that was it.

Mitchell kept going. He banged his against a shelf. It was Angel's class Angel's castle was in the middle.

At home he had fallen over it. bashed in the tower.

By accident.

Angel came down the hall. "My ca like a gas station," she said. "All y Her eyes watered.

"I'm sorry." Mitchell pulled at T-shirt. His grandmother had giv Nana thought he was Number On

Angel said he was Number Ei

Now kids were pounding down the stairs.

Mr. Oakley raced by. He was the grandfather who helped out.

"Are you going to Afternoon Center?" Habib asked.

Mitchell leaned away from Habib's poison-ivy arm. "I have to go," he said. "My mother signed my slip. All because of Angel."

Angel was getting to be a real tattletale.

Then Mitchell remembered. "My slip is still upstairs. It's in my desk."

He saw Angel in a doorway. She was watching him. Frowning.

"I have to get my slip," he told Habib.

He saw a mask on the floor. It had cut-out eyes and a clown nose.

He stuck the mask on his face. "Bonk," he said. "Bonk," Habib said back.

Mitchell headed for his classroom. He probably wasn't supposed to be there after school.

He kept the mask on. No one would know who he was.

The school might be filled with tattletales. Like Angel!

He threw his books out of his desk.

The slip was all the way in the back. It was crumpled up like Zelda A. Zigzag's face.

He went downstairs again. He barreled around Jake the Sweeper.

He dropped the mask on the bottom step.

"Hey," Jake said. "Don't make a mess."

Jake was a little grouchy.

So was his cat, Terrible Thomas.

Terrible Thomas sneaked into school sometimes.

Mitchell put the mask on a table in the hall.

Habib was standing next to the table. "You should see the sign-up line," he said. "It's like a jungle fight. Everyone wants to be first."

"Not me." Mitchell peeked in at the gym.

Ms. Katz sat at a table.

She must be the boss of the Afternoon Center.

In front of her was a girl in Mitchell's class.

What was her name? Sumiko.

Her mother and father were from Japan.

It was in the Arctic Circle somewhere. Or maybe the equator. You couldn't drive there, anyway.

Sumiko was probably the smartest kid in the school. She knew seven Japanese words.

Hello. Goodbye. Your room is a mess.

Angel was stuck in line with Yolanda. They were standing behind that monster Peter Petway.

Mitchell hoped Angel was safe there.

He didn't want to go near Peter Petway.

"Let's go out to the schoolyard," he told Habib. "See what's going on."

"Why not?" Habib said.

Mitchell grabbed the mask. He followed Habib upstairs and out the door.

CHAPTER 3

STILL MONDAY

Outside, Ramón was playing ball with some of the kids. He was a helper from college.

Mitchell sank down against a wall. It was the end of summer. Even the bricks were hot.

He and Habib listened to the noise inside.

Mitchell put on the mask. He crawled over to the basement window.

He crawled carefully. Junk was all over the

ground. Crushed-up Doritos. Old pens. Ants.

Jake's cat, Terrible Thomas, was eating Doritos. Maybe he was eating ants, too.

Mitchell looked in the open window. It was covered with wire. Inside was the lunchroom.

Kids raced down the aisle. They dumped their backpacks on the tables.

The lunch lady came out with a tray. She wore a shower cap. Only her ears stuck out.

"Snacks?" Habib said. "No one told me about that."

"No one told me, either," Mitchell said.

He tried to see what was on the tray. They were probably healthy snacks.

But healthy snacks were better than nothing.

"I'm starving to death," he told Habib. "I haven't eaten since lunch."

It had been a terrible lunch. Cheese poppers, bread things with cheese stuck all over them. The cheese tasted like plastic.

Habib poked him with his arm. The poison-ivy arm.

"Look what they're giving out. The rest of the cheese poppers."

Yolanda looked up. "Hey. Someone with a mask! I think it's a robber."

Someone else screamed.

Not a robber, Mitchell thought. *A loser.*

That made him sad.

He backed away.

He and Habib crawled to another window.

They looked in at the storeroom. It was filled with old desks.

Angel was hopping across the desks. She waved her skinny arms. It was a good thing Ms. Katz wasn't around to see her.

Angel looked up and screamed.

Mitchell jumped. The mask!

Angel would be having nightmares tonight. Screaming like a baboon.

He sighed and lifted the mask. "It's just me. And Habib."

"Whew." She stopped hopping.

"Did you sign up for the Center?" She narrowed her eyes. "Mom said—"

"Don't worry." Mitchell crossed his fingers. "I'm in."

"You don't look in to me." She waved her arms. "I'm practicing. Afternoon Center has swimming. It's at the Y."

She leaped across a desk. "They're giving prizes. Next Monday. I want to win one."

A prize! He'd never won a prize. Not unless you counted a monkey on a stick. He'd won it at the carnival.

It had fallen apart in two minutes.

What if he could win a prize?

That monster Peter Petway would say he was terrific.

"Let's go sign up," he told Habib.

They went into the gym.

Ms. Katz smiled. "I thought you'd forgotten."

She looked at the slip. "Your mother signed you up for a lot of things."

It wasn't his mother. It was Angel.

First his mom had signed the slip. Then Angel must have filled in a bunch of stuff.

"Ballroom dancing." Ms. Katz poked at her glasses. "Nature. Swimming. Opera? Can you sing?"

Wait till he saw Angel.

"I'll put a check next to Homework Help," Ms. Katz said. "You could use it. And you, too, Habib."

They rushed to the lunchroom.

A girl from his class was helping out.

Mitchell remembered. Her name was Destiny Washington. On Friday she'd had a braid down her back.

Today she had a white stripe in her bangs. She looked like a friendly skunk.

"My mother is a hairdresser," she had told him.

Destiny gave Habib four poppers. She gave Mitchell only three. "I'm running out," she said. "Sorry."

"Don't worry," Mitchell said.

"Hold your nose while you eat," Habib told him. "You won't smell the plastic."

Mitchell held his nose with two fingers. He took a bite. "It works!" he told Habib.

He sat there and chewed. Maybe the prize was a gold medal. Or silver.

Maybe it was a trip to Japan . . . right around the icebergs.

He might take Angel with him. "You're the best," she'd say.

But how could you win if you weren't good at anything?

How could you win if you were a loser?

Even Angel kept calling him Number Eighty-seven.

He shoved another popper in his mouth.

He had to think of something.

CHAPTER 4

TUESDAY

Mitchell stopped to look at Angel's castle.

She had painted it gold. Lumpy gold.

Now it looked worse than a gas station.

It could be a landing dock for UFOs.

Two kindergarten kids stood in the doorway. They chopped the air with their hands.

"I'm Trevor, the Karate Kid," one of them said.

Mitchell jumped. Then he saw that Trevor was crying. "What's the matter?"

"My mask is gone," the boy said.

Mitchell swallowed. "Did it have a clown nose?"

"Yes. It made me look tough. Just like Zelda A. Zigzag." The boy sniffled. "I wrote my initials on the back. *T.P.*, for Trevor Petway."

Mitchell gulped. "Peter Petway is your brother?"

Trevor nodded.

Mitchell closed his eyes. "Did you tell him about the mask?"

"Good idea," Trevor said.

"Don't do that," Mitchell said quickly. "Couldn't you make another one?"

"I'd need scissors and markers. All that stuff."

The other kid punched at the air. "It's tough to make those masks. Mine's great. It says *C.D.* for Clifton Dunbar right on the teeth."

"Don't worry, Trevor," Mitchell said. "I'll find it."

"Thanks." Trevor and Clifton gave each other high fives.

Mitchell headed for the lunchroom. How could he have lost that mask? And what if Peter Petway found out about it?

"Don't forget Homework Help," Ms. Katz called from the end of the hall.

What next!

Hot dogs were left over from lunch. Now they were cut in half.

Destiny handed them out. "I'm the lunch lady's helper." She gave two hot dogs to Mitchell. She gave one to Habib. "It's only fair. Habib got an extra last time."

Mitchell ate one. He took the other to

Homework Help. He had to work on a story of his life so far.

He'd use the hot dog for an eraser. He always made mistakes.

Ellie, the other college helper, smiled at him. She looked like a TV star. She had three tiny freckles.

"I'm the homework helper," she said.

Only a couple of kids were there.

Mitchell sat down next to Habib.

Habib was staring up at the ceiling. "I have to add stuff. Seven apples and six oranges. I don't have enough fingers."

"Use your tongue," Mitchell said. "That's what my father told me."

"Excellent idea," said Ellie.

"Yes," Mitchell said. It really didn't work. His tongue always got mixed up.

Ellie leaned over. She began to count with Habib.

Mitchell opened his notebook. He was glad he had to write about his life so far. It was easier than math. He took a bite of the hot dog. Then he began.

I used to be in another school.

Angel's room was far away.

She had no friends in my class.

She didn't know what I was doing.

Mitchell read it over. *Good work so far,* he told himself in Ms. Katz's voice.

He erased some marks on the paper with the hot dog. Then he bounced it off the table. It landed on Habib's paper.

Habib bounced the hot dog back.

"We could win a prize for bouncing hot dogs," Mitchell said.

Ellie laughed. She looked at her watch. "Enough for today."

She plastered a sticker on Mitchell's shirt.

It was a killer rabbit. She gave one to Habib, too.

"Come back tomorrow," she said.

"I guess so," Mitchell said.

Out in the hall, he and Habib ran into a hundred kids.

Some were on their way to the gym. Some peeled off at the art room.

Mrs. Farelli was the art teacher.

She was almost as tough as Zelda A. Zigzag.

Mitchell inched his way along. He kept his eyes open for the mask.

He hoped it wasn't on the floor. It would look as if a cow had run over it.

In the gym, Sumiko was swinging on a rope. She was almost to the ceiling. "I know two other words," she called. "*Mother* and *father*."

Sumiko would probably win a trip to Japan.

Mitchell would have to cross that prize off his list.

Terrible Thomas, the cat, had sneaked in again. Mitchell hopped over him.

Thomas swiped out his paw.

"Yeow!" Mitchell yelled.

Mitchell looked into the music room. *"Meeee meeeee meee,"* a girl sang. She sounded like a singing chicken.

She wore a loopy pearl thing around her neck. It hung down to her waist.

"That's Gina from my class," Habib said. "She wants to win a prize for opera."

The music teacher held his head. Maybe he had a toothache.

Mitchell knew he wouldn't win a prize for singing. He sang like his dog, Maggie.

The music teacher saw them. "Come on in."

They walked into the room. Slowly.

Everyone began to sing. Mitchell sang without making a sound.

Tomorrow Mr. Oakley was taking them to the nature center. That would be better than singing.

He was going to give nature his best try.

CHAPTER 5

WEDNESDAY

Mitchell ate his snack in one gulp. It was string cheese. His favorite.

He had to hurry. He was late for Homework Help.

No one was there except Habib. And Ellie.

Habib had taken off his sneakers. He must be counting on his toes.

Mitchell wrote in a quick burst:

Sometimes losers should get a pris.
It would make them feel good.

Ellie leaned over. "What's a pris?"

Mitchell slapped his forehead. "Prize."

He pulled out the hot dog. Too bad it was falling apart.

He erased the *s*. He wrote *z*.

"Excellent," Ellie said. "Just stick an *e* on the end. You're all set."

He wrote a little more.

Then it was time for the nature center. He raced upstairs with Habib. They passed Peter Petway. He was heading for the gym.

That reminded Mitchell. He'd heard Angel talking to Yolanda. "I hate to walk home with Mitchell," she'd said. Now Yolanda must think he was a loser, too.

Habib poked him. "Come on."

They shot outside. Just in time!

Ramón led the line. Mr. Oakley came next.

Mr. Oakley said he was in love with nature.

Angel and Yolanda were up in front with Destiny.

Today Destiny's hair was green. "In honor of nature," she said.

Habib was juggling. He scrambled for the balls.

Mr. Oakley walked to the end of the line.

He walked with Mitchell. "Hello there," he said.

Mitchell liked the look of Mr. Oakley. He had puffs of hair coming out of his ears. Like little earmuffs.

"Up ahead is the Steven Z. Zigzag Nature Center," said Mr. Oakley.

"Maybe that's Zelda Zigzag's husband," Mitchell said.

"You're right! I see you're a thinker," Mr. Oakley said.

Too bad Angel hadn't heard that.

They walked up a skinny path. "Look." Mr. Oakley pointed toward the bushes. "Don't go close."

Mitchell hoped it wasn't a pack of wild animals. Maybe coyotes. They could be hiding in the weeds.

They'd bite your leg right off.

Was a nature prize worth having to walk around with just one leg?

Angel was right next to the bushes. In danger.

He darted up to her. He pushed her out of the way. She landed in a pile of bushes.

Angel gave him her worst look. A pushed-up nose and squinty eyes.

"Sorry," Mitchell said.

Mr. Oakley helped her up. "I was going to tell you. Those plants are poison ivy. So don't touch. See? Three leaves, shiny green." He shook his head. "You can get an itchy rash. Better wash when you get home."

"I have poison ivy in my yard," Habib said. He sounded proud.

Mr. Oakley looked at Habib's arm. "So I see."

Habib was probably going to win the nature prize, Mitchell thought.

Mr. Oakley bent over. Mitchell hoped he wouldn't fall into the poison ivy, too. He started forward.

Before Mitchell could save him, Mr. Oakley stood up. "Here is one of my favorite creatures." He pointed at the ground.

All Mitchell saw was a skinny worm.

"A worm!" Mr. Oakley sounded as if he had just opened a treasure chest.

Mitchell tried to look as if he'd opened a treasure chest, too.

"They tunnel through the earth," Mr. Oakley said. "They make the soil fluffy. Plants have room to grow."

Like poison ivy, Mitchell thought.

"Now for the best part," said Mr. Oakley.

They walked about a hundred miles.

"I'm ready to fall on the ground," Habib said. "I don't think I'm a nature person."

"Me neither," Mitchell said. "Not if we have to walk till our feet fall off."

At last, they saw a bunch of trees. "Apple trees," said Mr. Oakley. "Take an apple."

"I'll take a couple," Habib said. "I'll juggle with them."

Everyone jumped up to pick apples.

Mitchell was too tired to jump. He scooped two apples off the ground. One for him. The other for Angel. To make up for the poison ivy.

"Don't take them from the ground," Mr. Oakley said.

It was too late. Mitchell bit into his apple . . .

Right into one of Mr. Oakley's favorite creatures.

He dropped the apple. The other half of the

favorite creature was still wiggling. "Sorry, worm," he said.

"Eww!" Angel spit out her bite of apple. She began to scream. She grabbed her throat. "I swallowed a worm!"

"Oh, no!" Yolanda yelled. "Angel's been poisoned!"

"I might end up in the hospital." Angel wiped her mouth hard.

She stared at Mitchell. "Because of you, Mitchell 'Number Eighty-seven' McCabe."

Mr. Oakley sighed. "You're all right. A worm won't hurt you."

Mitchell sighed, too.

He wasn't going to win a nature prize.

CHAPTER 6

THURSDAY

Mitchell stopped at the kindergarten shelf. He saw Clifton's mask. The mask had big teeth. There was a big *C* on one tooth. There was a *D* on the other.

But where was Trevor's mask?

Mitchell had to find it before Peter Petway found out he had lost it.

It wasn't on the stairs.

Maybe it was in the schoolyard.

Too bad it was raining outside. The Zelda A. Zigzag School smelled like his dog, Maggie.

Mitchell took another sniff. It smelled a little like his old school, too.

It was time to search. But now his raincoat had disappeared.

He never could find anything! Angel was right about that!

He'd go outside to look anyway.

He'd have to skip Homework Help. He'd have to skip Ellie with her three freckles.

What about snack?

He couldn't skip that. He'd have a hole in his stomach.

Mitchell dashed to the lunchroom. He was fast enough to be first in line for leftover pizza.

Habib was right behind him. They looked out the windows.

Habib twirled his hand around. "It's dark out there. Windy. It looks like a—a what-do-you-call-it?"

Mitchell frowned. "Something like a tomato." Wasn't that a big wind that carried people away?

Never mind. He still had to go outside. He had to find that mask.

He took a bite of pizza. It looked like cardboard. It tasted like cardboard, too.

"Could I have the pizza box?" Mitchell asked the lunch lady.

She tucked one ear in her shower cap. She handed him the box.

Mitchell took another pizza slice.

He went up the stairs and opened the door.

Wow! It was raining hard. He could hardly see the schoolyard. Maybe there was a flood. He might drown.

He went out anyway.

"Yeow." He held the box over his head. It made an almost-umbrella. He took a bite of pizza.

He splashed through the giant puddles. He looked for the mask. It wasn't in the playground area. It wasn't near the windows.

His #1 T-shirt was stuck to his back.

Pizza sauce ran down his face.

He jumped into the air. He landed in the mud.

It felt great.

Angel called from the storeroom window. "Is that blood all over you?" She sounded worried.

Mitchell sighed. "It's pizza sauce."

"You're going to be soaked. You can get sick from all that rain."

Mitchell checked behind the bushes. No mask. Just Terrible Thomas hiding from the rain.

"Miiiiitchell!" Angel screeched.

"I'm coming," he yelled.

"I won't even have a brother."

"I'm coming in right now." He dropped the pizza box into the litter basket.

In the hall, he shook himself like Maggie. Drops flew all over.

Ms. Katz stood there. She held his raincoat out with one finger. "Get a towel from the boys' room. Wipe yourself off."

Mitchell took his raincoat. "Thanks."

"It was in the lunchroom. Under a table." Ms. Katz sighed. "Everyone was stepping on it."

He remembered now. He had left it there at lunchtime.

Ms. Katz leaned forward. "I lose things, too. My gloves, my umbrella."

She grinned at Mitchell. Then she hurried away.

He went into the boys' room.

Trevor was looking at himself in the mirror. "Eeeee-*yah!*" he yelled.

Mitchell ducked out again. He had a terrible feeling about the mask.

He shivered. He wrapped his raincoat

around him. He was soaking wet and freezing.

He sat on the bottom step.

Peter Petway came down the stairs.

Mitchell hid his face. He certainly looked like a loser. He was covered with mud. And pizza sauce.

Peter jumped over him and ran off.

Then Mitchell thought about Angel.

Sometimes she surprised him.

She was worried about him.

That made him feel pretty good.

He sat up straight. Maybe he wasn't such a loser after all.

CHAPTER 7

FRIDAY

Last day of the week. Great!

Today the Afternoon Center kids were going swimming.

Mitchell had found his bathing suit before school. It was under his bed, still damp from the end of the summer.

It had a ton of sand in it.

He held it up to his nose. What a smell.

He hoped no one would notice.

He had forgotten his best lunch, too. A ham sandwich with enough lettuce for a rabbit.

Sumiko lent him money for hot lunch.

It was the worst lunch in the world: meat chunks in glue.

At last, the bell rang. The loudspeaker blared. "Time for swimming."

They headed for the bus line.

Mitchell let Habib cut in front of him.

Habib let Destiny cut in front of him.

Sumiko cut in front of Destiny.

And some kid stepped in between Destiny

and Sumiko. Mitchell thought his name might be Charlie.

Mitchell turned. Peter Petway was near the end of the line.

"Let's get moving," Peter said.

Mitchell hoped Peter didn't know he had started all that cutting.

The bus pulled up. The kids packed in like meat chunks in glue.

Angel and Yolanda sat in front of Mitchell and Habib. "What's that smell?" Yolanda asked.

"Someone's wet bathing suit," Angel said. "Eew."

Mitchell took his bathing suit bag off his lap. He sat on it.

He watched Angel practice swimming in her seat. "Here I come, prize," she said. She wiggled her arms.

Mitchell crossed his fingers. Maybe there were two prizes for swimming.

He wiggled his arms.

At last, they were there.

The boys went to one locker room. The girls went to another. Lockers banged. Everyone changed.

"Something smells around here," a boy said.

Mitchell didn't look up. It sounded like Peter Petway.

Mitchell raced out of the locker room.

He couldn't wait to get into the pool. It would wash away the smell of his bathing suit. It would get rid of that ton of sand.

"Great suit," Yolanda was telling Mr. Oakley.

Mitchell blinked. Mr. Oakley's bathing suit had zigzags. It came down to his knobby knees.

Sumiko wore a red bathing suit. Mitchell's favorite color.

Mitchell slid into the pool. "Yeow!" he yelled. It was up to his knees, and freezing.

They had to stay at the shallow end until they passed a swimming test.

Mitchell had to swim about a hundred miles to pass. He'd probably sink any minute.

But Mr. Oakley blew his whistle. "A-one effort, Mitchell," he said. "You passed."

Mitchell floated along, catching his breath. Then he went down to the bottom. He pretended he was a stingray.

He opened his eyes.

What were all those tan dots?

He shot up. His mouth was filled with water. So was his nose.

He tried to breathe.

Then he spotted Angel.

She had sunk to the bottom, too.

She might not be a stingray. She might be drowning.

He grabbed her mouse tail hair. He yanked hard.

She came up sputtering. She waded away.

Mr. Oakley blew his whistle. "No ducking, pushing, or pulling, guys," he called. "Safety first."

Mitchell began to swim across the pool.

The other side was far away.

Very far away.

He scrunched down. He
waved his arms. He walked
across the bottom.

"Good job. You swam half-
way," Ellie said. "I'll give you
a great sticker tomorrow."

Mitchell knew it wasn't a good job.
Swimming with your feet on the bottom wasn't
really A-1.

Habib sat at the side of the pool. "Too bad I
can't go in," he said. "Not with poison ivy."

Mitchell waved to Sumiko. She was sitting
on the high diving board. "I know the Japanese
word for *water*," she yelled down.

Mitchell tried to swim again. But his arms
were tired. He turned
over and floated.

Kids were splash-
ing. Peter Petway was
swimming underwater.
Mitchell waded away
from him.

Hey. Where was Angel?

What if she had drowned? He wouldn't have a sister.

He dived down. She wasn't there.

She wasn't anywhere.

Then he saw her. Whew!

She was sitting behind a post. Was she hiding? Why was she there all by herself?

CHAPTER 8

SATURDAY

Mitchell thought the Afternoon Center would be closed on Saturday.

It wasn't, though.

Not everyone was there. Some kids had other things to do.

But Mitchell didn't have one thing to do. Neither did Habib.

Mitchell was a little sorry Ellie was there. He'd have to go to Homework Help.

Almost no one else ever went. Just him. And Habib.

Mitchell didn't want Ellie to be lonely.

He went in and began to write:

Saturday was a day off in my old school.
It was locked up.
Sometimes I liked that.
Sometimes I didn't.

Ramón came into the room. He was always carrying a math book.

He was studying math in college.

Today Ramón and Habib were going to work on numbers.

Mitchell shook his head. Ramón wasn't so smart.

He should have learned numbers by fifth grade. Even Peter Petway must know all that stuff by now.

Mitchell kept writing.

Habib was counting under his breath.

Ellie began to talk to Ramón. She looked happy.

"You can go now," she told Mitchell and Habib. She stuck flower stickers on their shirts.

In the hall, Mitchell and Habib looked at each other. "Flowers!" Habib said.

They peeled the stickers off.

They went down the hall to the art room.

On the way, Mitchell looked for Trevor's mask.

He found crumbs from yesterday's lunch.

But no mask.

Mrs. Farelli waved to them from her desk. She had art stuff all over the place.

Yolanda was drawing a picture. Maybe it was a lion. Mitchell asked her.

She shook her head. "No, it's Terrible Thomas."

"Good drawing," Mitchell said.

What could he work on?

He had a great idea.

You're a thinker, he said to himself in a Mr. Oakley voice.

Angel came into the room. She took paper and colored pencils to an easel.

Angel liked to draw.

Habib found a box of rubber bands. He jumbled them into a ball. "Good for juggling," he said.

Mitchell folded a piece of cardboard into four parts.

Angel looked over his shoulder. "What are you doing?"

"Guess."

"Making stairs?" Angel asked.

"Guess again." Mitchell glued the edges together.

"Why do you always stick your tongue out?" Angel said. "You look like Maggie."

Mitchell didn't mind looking like Maggie. She was a good dog.

He found sparkly gold paint.

Angel began to smile. "I know. It's a tower for my castle."

"Right," said Mitchell.

He dumped gold paint all over it.

He and Angel went to her shelf.

Mitchell's hands were sticky. So was the tower.

It dripped all over the floor. Right onto a bunch of crumbs. They looked like gold nuggets.

Wait until Jake the Sweeper saw them.

Mitchell rubbed the dots with his feet.

One dot with his right foot.

Another dot with his left.

"Watch out," Angel said.

Bonk!

Mitchell tripped across the floor.

The tower flew into Peter Petway.

Double bonk!

"The tower is ruined!" Angel said. "I can't believe it."

Peter Petway was sitting on the floor. He was covered in gold dots.

"I've been looking for you," Peter said.

Uh-oh! Mitchell closed his eyes.

He thought about his old school.

Nothing scary like this ever happened there.

CHAPTER 9

STILL SATURDAY

Peter Petway leaned forward.

Mitchell leaned back.

"Why did you call my brother a loser?" Angel put her hands on her hips. "I saw you from the window that day."

Mitchell grabbed her arm. Who knew what Peter Petway would do?

Peter blinked. "Not me." He shook his head.

"That's what I call my brother, Trevor. He calls me that, too."

Mitchell let out his breath.

Up close, Peter didn't look so tough.

But Angel had her worst look: a pushed-up nose and squinty eyes. "Why are you looking for my brother?" she asked.

Wow. Angel was tough.

Peter ducked into a classroom. "Wait," he called. "I'll be right back."

He came out with Trevor's mask. "Someone said you were looking for a mask."

What a mess it was. Mitchell rubbed it on his shirt. "Thanks," he said. "It belongs to Trevor."

Mitchell turned the mask over. Hadn't Peter seen Trevor's *T.P.*?

"Look," Angel said. "He wrote his initials backwards. *P.T.* instead of *T.P.*"

They all grinned at each other.

Peter gave them each a high five. Then he disappeared into the gym.

"I have to look for Trevor," Mitchell told Angel.

Trevor found them first. He jumped out of the boys' room. "Eeeee-*yaaah!*" he yelled.

He stopped. "Did I scare you?"

"Yes!" Angel said.

Trevor looked happy. "I might win a prize for karate."

Mitchell held out the mask.

Trevor gave the clown nose a pat. "I knew you'd find it."

It was time to go home for lunch. Mitchell and Angel started down the path.

Mr. Oakley was outside. He took a bag out of his pocket. Inside was a squashed sandwich.

Mitchell sniffed. It smelled like peanut butter. It made his stomach rumble.

"It's for the squirrels." Mr. Oakley left it on the front lawn.

Jake the Sweeper would have a fit.

"It makes the squirrels happy," Mr. Oakley said. "It makes me happy, too."

"You're very good at nature," Mitchell said.

Mr. Oakley laughed. "Everyone is good at something."

He went down Plum Street. "Don't forget," he said. "Monday is prize day."

Terrible Thomas, the cat, flew out of the bushes. He scarfed down half the sandwich.

Mitchell and Angel headed for home.

"I'm not going to win a prize," Angel said. "I'm not good at anything."

Mitchell was surprised. He thought she was good at everything.

"You're a good swimmer." He crossed his fingers.

"I sink right to the bottom," she said.

"Well . . ."

She leaned closer. "Listen, Mitchell. I saw specks in the pool. Maybe seeds."

She scratched her arm. "They might grow into sharks."

Sharks!

But then Mitchell shook his head. "I don't think sharks grow in pools."

"How about lizards?"

"Maybe not." He took a breath. "I'm not good at anything, either."

"But Mr. Oakley said everyone is good at something."

Mitchell saw a worm on the sidewalk.

He picked it up. He put it in a puddle.

Monday he'd ask Mr. Oakley about sharks and lizards. He'd find out where they grew.

Mitchell opened their side door. "Wait. I just thought of something."

Angel stopped.

"I know what the seeds were," he said. "Sand from my bathing suit."

"Really?" Angel smiled. "You're shaping up, Mitchell. You're beginning to think. And something else," she said.

He wouldn't win a prize for thinking. But still it was a good thing to do.

"Yolanda says you're an okay kid."

He couldn't believe it. An okay kid. Wow!

He thought of poor Angel. Good at nothing.

He thought a little more.

"You're good at being a sister," he said.

Angel grinned. "Too bad I can't get a prize for that."

"Yes," Mitchell said. "But a being a good sister isn't bad at all."

CHAPTER 10

MONDAY—PRIZE DAY

Mitchell wore his I'M #1 shirt.

It wasn't Number One anymore. It had cheese-popper stains and mud stains. It had pizza stains, too.

Mom had put it in the washing machine. Mitchell had pulled it out before it got wet.

After school, he followed everyone to the lunchroom.

The lunch lady's face was red. "I've been working on a special snack. It's prize day, you know."

Mitchell wondered what the snack was. It might be horrible.

Something like chicken livers.

It wasn't, though.

The lunch lady brought out blueberry muffins.

All of them had a *1* on top.

"It's because of your shirt," the lunch lady told Mitchell.

Habib grinned at him. So did Sumiko and Destiny.

Destiny gave Mitchell two muffins. "It's only fair," she said.

"Thanks." He ate the blueberries out of the tops. Then he and Habib went down to Homework Help.

Next to him, Habib counted aloud. "One hundred forty-eight plus eighty-one . . ."

"You're getting good at this," Mitchell said.

". . . equals almost five hundred," Habib said.

Mitchell found his pencil. He began to write.

**The Zelda A. Zigzag School is
Number One.
I'm glad to be here.
Even without a prize.**

They went to the auditorium. Ms. Katz was sitting on the stage.

She looked different.

Mitchell wondered why.

Then Gina sang "The Star-Spangled Banner."

Ms. Katz stood up. "That's our first prize," she said. "It's to Gina for good strong singing."

Gina twirled her pearl necklace. She went up to the stage for a looks-like-gold medal.

Everyone clapped.

Ms. Katz looked around. She frowned.

Mitchell saw why she looked different. She had sat on her glasses.

Yolanda pointed. Then Ms. Katz saw the glasses on her chair. She looked at Mitchell and smiled.

"We have a medal for Yolanda for artwork," she said. "And one for Destiny. She helps out with snacks."

"I have yellow zigzags in my hair today," Destiny said. "It's in honor of Zelda A. Zigzag."

Ms. Katz gave out a million more prizes.

That kid named Charlie got one for helping Jake the Sweeper.

Mitchell kept his head down. He wouldn't get anything.

Neither would Habib and Angel.

Then Ms. Katz called Habib's name.

"This medal is for juggling with one apple," Ms. Katz said. "Good work, Habib."

Habib came back to his seat. "Next week I'll try to juggle with two apples."

Next was Sumiko. It was because she knew Japanese words!

She had taught Mitchell one of them. *Hai.*

It meant—

Mitchell had to think.

"Yes!"

Ms. Katz said, "We have one more medal. It's for Angel McCabe."

Angel!

Mitchell tried to think. Angel couldn't swim. She was afraid of everything. Her castle looked like—

"Everyone makes castles with towers," Ms. Katz said. "Angel made one that's different. So this is for imagination."

Mitchell clapped hard. His hands stung.

Angel came back to her seat. "I'm glad you smashed the castle," she told Mitchell. "Maybe you're Number One after all."

Then Ellie climbed up to the stage. "I want to give out a prize, too." She smiled at Mitchell.

Mitchell sat up straight.

Was he good at something besides thinking?

"Mitchell gets a prize for writing."

Mitchell ran up onto the stage.

"Excellent work, Mitchell." Ellie pinned a medal to his shirt.

Everyone clapped. Mitchell felt great. Better than that. He felt excellent.

"What about me?" a voice called.

"Me too," said another.

Everyone looked around.

"Trevor and Clifton!" Ms. Katz said.

They went up to the stage.

"Medals? Of course!" Ms. Katz said. "You win for making masks."

"Eee-*yaaah!*" said Trevor. He grinned at Clifton.

Mitchell sat back. He looked at his medal. It had been the best day.

But then he saw Angel's arm.

Poison ivy! It must be from the nature walk.

Bonk!

Angel would probably figure that out.

He'd be right back to Number Eighty-seven again.

But for now, he was Number One.

More afternoon fun
for everyone at
the Zigzag School!